KB067471

Thinking Less about Sad Things

Thinking Less about Sad Things

Sad Things

A collection of new poems by Moon Dong-man
Translated by Brother Anthony of Taizé

Contents

THINKING LESS
ABOUT SAD THINGS

Cooking Rice

Thanks to you going to prepare rice

I stayed alive,

thanks to the grains

washed with earth-stained hands.

Thanks to the people going to prepare rice,

we just about managed to stay alive,

thanks to fingers worked to the bone to obtain

the rice,

thanks to the wrinkled labor

lighting a fire in the fire pit and basking in the

smoke,

Thanks to the deep rice paddle,

thanks to lives humble

as the water draining away in the sink.

Thanks to lives
unable to live for as long as it takes
to bring the water to the boil,
we stayed alive.

So...
Saying go home and cook rice
is to say I'm not worth stale rice
is to say I should throw rice away
is to say I'm not rice's child
is to say I'm not a family member of charcoal smoke.

Gaining a Rib

I was riding a bicycle when the handlebars snapped and I went soaring up into the air. Then I flopped back down onto the ground like a bird that has smashed into a window, and I felt so faint that I could not think of my way home. Both the surroundings and my mind grew dark, I could faintly hear people chattering, cypress trees or poplar fences, people on the way to market, on the way to catch a bus, on the way to buy medicine, footsteps stopped, those stopped footsteps seem to rescue my stopping breath.

As they diverted traffic, called an ambulance, made me talk, asked who I was, they were noisy but low-pitched breaths. As the challenged veins turned into blood like water, I must have longed for words questioning me. Who were those women that I can't even remember?

Might it have been my sister? My mother or a classmate? Maybe it was the lady serving out food at the restaurant or those busy Eves selling yogurt. They were protecting my cracked ribs for quite as long as it would take to eat supper.

Thinking as I lay on the cold but not so sad ground, the thought that the claim that the first woman was made by culling one of Adam's ribs might be a cracked hypothesis. That was an evening when I got into the ambulance with the help of a woman much smaller than me who came running,

permeating into the enlightenment of a cozy fall,

and gained a rib, while even the sound of the siren

was music.

Inside

After the woman finally left the house

there was a rumor that it was a relief

that the person who had to leave had gone.

The one left single cared for

the two dogs she left behind.

To feed just those two dogs,

he rouses his skinny body at dawn,

lights an endless cigarette

and after scooping up a few spoonfuls of plain rice

he fills a bowl for the sticky-eyed pair.

Since he forgot how to divide a load by balancing

left and right,

As he slings his toolbag over a collapsing
right shoulder,
the dogs wag tails of sorrow mixed with moans
like a parting between close relatives.

Again and again he closes the door,
then opens it again,
and some days, he just closes the door.

While it seems there were also days
when he came back inside.

Dream Forest Nursing Home

I'm lying down. In a 6-person ward
I can't get up unassisted
and the only part of nature I can see lying down is
clouds,
   the only thing that glimmers and shakes is a skate-
shaped kite

My symptoms have grown serious. Beyond the
window
   that my caregiver opens sometimes, I hear people
chattering,
   dogs barking.

It reminds me of a spring day when willow trees
sprout new leaves.

I recall the low stone wall of a tiled house

where I'm sure decent people lived,

the lover who sang serenades,

we would turn the corner of the bamboo forest

after gnawing Phoenix tree fruit

and kissed briefly

And there was a beautiful pond

where our youth flowed and pooled, and as we counted

the many kinds of clouds suspended on the mountain ridge

you and I were in our footsteps, our palms warm

because we were holding each other's hands.

My sour-smelling body still remembers
the moments of love.

I hope you are not lying somewhere
looking like me.

I can see a kite outside the window.
I have become as small as I was when I flew a kite
with my father.
I don't have a mom, but I'm Mum's baby again,
burbling nonsense like an infant babbling,

Now someone changes my diapers and feeds me
watery gruel,
and these days, never seen, undreamed of,

will gradually disappear like a kite with a broken
string.

Once I have become a green unmarked grave,
finally with no dream or reality.

And someone will fly a green kite,
with no one knowing it's my memories,
it's my grave.

Continuing Days

On cleaning the rafters black with smoke from
the fireplace,
   a perfect pattern appeared from under the soot,
   like the structure of a poem that never grows old,
   like dignity.

Whatever newness there may be
is bound to grow old and collapse.
   The people who say it's new aren't particularly new
either.

   The history of houses
   where everything disappears except for the
foundations
   is not a question of what might get left behind,

not a question of how it might make a leap forward

while it's being lived in and used,

but rather a matter of going on being used without

collapsing.

Rather than a flawless house that needs no repairs,

an old house shored up,

with a suitable piece of wood,

supporting a worm eaten, rotten pillar

that barely stands as it is,

is more like a new house,

like a poem.

When I finally disappear one day,

after being cast aside, barely surviving, kept alive,

I think it's appropriate

that even my dependent poetry should finally

disappear.

Everything written becoming waste paper,

collapsing, leaving behind a simple stone, neither

embossed nor engraved,

such a dramatic bankruptcy

is surely the legacy of poetry?

There's poetry in an old house.

There's a house that should be demolished in

poetry.

A Goshawk

A goshawk was turning in the sky.

A boy is turning all day long outside a doorless
door.

He can't open the door that isn't there.

The inside is scary and the outside is cold.

It has no place to rest, no prey to fold its wings

and peck at.

Turning, because the world outside is warmer,

warming his hands with his breath,

he put his aching feet

on the footprints of his family heading inward)

Some feet are afraid

while a woman's scaly, cracked feet are pitiful.

A little girl's feet look so cold
he longs to rub them for a long time.
Fine cracks have developed in some feet
after leaving home and hearing nothing.

An evening when the smoke from the chimney is
smarting
and sorrowful water cooking rice is boiling,
all the boy can do is sweep the snow
with his toes,

Gathering up cold snow,
covering and warming his family's footprints
that have turned to ice,
while his feet freeze.

An Orphan

There were times when the word orphan sounded good. There were days when it would have been better if I had been a child rescued from under a bridge. Mother's legs were dry, exfoliating like snake scales. Did a woman who breathes hard like that without flesh give birth to me, and what became of her breasts that I used to touch then go to sleep every day? Where did the smell of smoke from her hair and the fragrant smell of face-powder vanish? You must have decided to make an orphan of me on the first day of the New Year, as you lay wearily beside the meal table after eating nothing but a few spoonfuls of gruel. When our eyes met, you weakly stretched out a rough hand like a ginseng stalk and grabbed my hand, eyes brimming with tears as if

I was someone you'd never see again, and spoke, a lifetime contained in those tight wrinkles round your eyes. You always had sore eyes, so is that why finally you just gave me those sore eyes as you departed? Should I call it a farewell, the brand your gaze left an arrow with no direction imprinted on my breast like a bird's foot print? Once your eyes had left my eyes and could not look back, should I call that being an orphan? Finally, being an orphan, I was no longer lonely. I was able to laugh more, like a madman. I had no time to be sad. I have been living the laughter you couldn't live laughing, that's the mission of an orphan, the waste of oozing eyes.

The Last Soybean Field

"I'll sow just once more, then leave it idle." Elderly mothers always lie. Just once more always means until the body is completely wrecked. The ground encouraged the bean stalks to wind round mother and not let go. Harvesting beans from her soybean field only separates Mother from her land for a short time.

The one whose pods open first, the one hiding in the shade, still green, the one with nothing on it because only the leaves were thick, all harvested and laid out in the yard like us stupid brothers. My wrist holding the sickle trembled like your tremor, as if I had lost all the strength the ground had given me. You said that you would leave this house, to which even your youngest child would never return, once the harvest is over, but knowing that it is a fantasy that flips over and over like a child's fickle dream, what should I sow to harden the yard that turns into a muddy field when the ground freezes that will boldly sprout? I had to finish the harvest while figuring out how to get rid of your muddy feet, who walk bent-backed to the sound of your asthmatic, rattling breath.

I hope that this small vegetable garden will not grow old as a fallow waste, that in spring the garlic leaves will lean in the sea breeze, and in summer the perilla leaves and corn stalks will surround it like a fence and never cease to hide the sad history of this house. In autumn, may the soybeans and black beans fill the pods out, and survive in this world.

May there be a magic trick so that her back, once straightened, will never bend again when an elderly mother drives in sticks to support the green peas.

When Mother picks out the black beans and puts them into my rice bowl, when my deaf mother's ears open, and we, mother and son, cry then smile, exchanging real words, if only what can't happen in this bean field now came back just once, and I wondered what crime it would be if time ran backwards just once and the days of green beans that lived together in a pod came back to life again.

Thinking Less about Sad Things

Mom...

went off to a world with no bean fields.

She left peas behind.

I...

cooked rice with beans without any rice.

Enjoy your meal

and live like a green bean,

thinking less about sad things.

A Dolmen

I set up a small stone in front of my parents'
shared grave
and carved on it the names of their children and
grandchildren,
their daughters' children first.

As I've grown older,
I've felt increasingly sorry for the women of this
world.

Since the good women left earlier,
I included the name of my sister
who left to be at Mom's side a long time ago,
before Mom.

Finally, the run-down tribe without a chief

was expanding its wealth

by a small stone grave.

In the distant future.

if people excavate it, they will think

it must be because we were herbivores

that never thrust a stone spear into innocent flesh

that we had no canine teeth.

It's not that we didn't have good times,

so that we could gather food peacefully.

I went into the forest with my mom,

we filled up all our pockets with ripe chestnuts

and when we left the forest,

our white sneakers used to have grass stains all over them.

In that small forest, somewhere to the south,
the stone tombs of ancestors who had come in as migrants
were clustered,

That brief moment of paradise
as I spread chestnuts moist with dew
on the warm stones.

What kind of materials should we gather
if we have to draw pictures of hunting?

Birthday

Just when frost was falling, as Mom went into labor,

Grandmother must have tightened her bun, inserted a hairpin,

crouched her aching back down by the fire pit,

broken pine branches and lit them.

The heated water must have washed me

and slowly seeped between dry, cracked lips.

In the early morning, when there was no house with lights on,

a frost-nipped cabbage got plump with its cold rim,

a hen clucked on a perch, then laid a warm egg,

the poor harvest managed to produce thin milk,

that there must have been a little mouth tirelessly

sucking.

Those labor pains, those frosty pains one late-autumn dawn,

while you gathered combings from a bamboo brush,

put them in a crack on the mud wall, with big and gentle eyes,

carrying things on your head or back like an ox,

your hair ever smelling of smoke, you who used to cry a lot,

must have spotted my forehead one day at dawn.

Is that why, today at dawn, gray-haired now,

I woke several times and tossed that dawn about

although my stomach wasn't aching?

Married Couple Washing their Feet

Thirty years since the two of us last walked a long
mountain path,
  we sat beside a stream,
  our toes facing each other.

As two feet touch,
twenty toes rub,
muddy water at once flows away,
incisions in water,
salty tears early one morning…
all mix and settle, then flow clearly.

When our toes shake, the water shakes.
As the water seems to fold and spread,
it too has deep wrinkles.

It's a day when I want to give birth to something.

It's a day when I want to give birth to one more
flowing word,

water-wrinkle, that's not even in the dictionary.

The trees of October, backs holding the sunlight,

the greenery that we still like.

The mountaintop leaves seem to be ageing already,

their ears are dry and red.

Troublesome little creatures like crayfish,

know it's time to reach a tributary and live under
a big stone

but now they've been playfully biting our toes.

Even if the only thing I built after coming here

was a blister, it can't burst,

a blister that I have proudly to take back home.

Maybe what built that blister

was our feet walking together with different feet?

Or the current tossing and turning?

Graffitti on a Bench Guided by a Dog

From an oak tree that has lived longer than me,
an acorn falls and goes rolling quietly.

Our white puppy sniffed at the acorn
then gave up, deciding it was inedible.

There are things I'm picky about, too, so I don't
bend,
   I don't get upset by food and the thought
   comes rolling that I'm lucky
   to have rolled all the way here.

We lie down on the bench, eat and forget steamed
chestnuts.
   I reflect that the puppy who likes chestnuts more

than I do

looks more human.

Eating, forgetting? I forget where that comes
from.

A dictionary? Some kind of pocket?

From a womb? Or a storeroom?

Biting words at every word, humming to draw
together

clouds that scatter and gather.

Lying on a low wooden bench, the single sound
'pyeong'

in Korean can mean Flat, Equal, Peace,

Composure, Serenity, Prairie.

as well as your son's flat feet.

Words that need to be spread widely,

words that seem to come and then go away,

I forget.

Graffitti on a Bench Guided by a Dog 2

Compared to you with your short leash,

my leash is just a little longer.

A Bell Ringing

The same sound comes surging like ripples,
always making a different sound.

Surging in, then leaving cherry blossom
rolling like butterflies round the yard.

Pooling lonesome, colliding lonesome,
it makes the sound that travels farthest.

It's a sound, but it leaves silence in its wake.
It gives birth to days
when I wake up without being surprised.

In the bell sound, there's no sound
of sin striking or of sorrow taking a beating.

You said it'd be nice to go inside

and live there, like a herbivore's fence.

This world's weary sounds all strive to be first

to go in.

In Musugol*

I think I lived here in some past life,

cultivating a small rice paddy and a vegetable
garden,

watching a pair of mandarin ducks,

making ripples of leisurely love in a flooded paddy
field,

sitting on the paddy field bank, smoking a
cigarette because I'm bored.

There's a surface in that small rice paddy, too.

There are waves, and there is stillness.

The wind drives the fallen cherry blossom to one
side,

* A small village with rice paddies at the foot of Dobongsan
Mountain in Seoul.

making a beautiful flower island.

There are several well-kept tombs across the stream,
  so that looking at this side from over there,
  I was able to think about my life,

While smelling the white bridal wreath blooming,
  as it wraps around a chestnut tree that's dying of old age and sickness.

Thinking about the great life known as repetition
  measuring life by death
  estimating not-dying by death,

Planting rice seedlings, digging up taro every year,

watching the person I love come walking from

afar,

I would have spread still smoldering ashes

over the chives field.

Like an old dog

When I come back from the island, I don't just
remember the island,

I also remember the old dog guarding all alone
the isolated house,

the owner of which has been away for a long time.

Even the battered, salt-crusted dog bowl,
I don't know who fills it up, but it's never empty,
is a lonesome great sight.

When I leave the island that is so like the old dog,

that at the sound of the ship's whistle
goes and lies down in the shade of a camellia tree,
its eyes, dried by the sea breeze. brimming with

tears.

Some people look ahead at the unknown waves
from the boat's prow,
   some look back at the vanishing current from the
stern.

But I belong to neither category,
cannot tear my eyes away.

But why
do both yearning and waves
go leaping along with front paws held high?

A leash

Two dogs died with their noses
in a bowl of frozen water,
lying there side by side
as if each other's body temperature was all they
could depend on.

A few steps away, indoors all was quiet,
where the kind owner who took care of feeding
them once lived,

The leash they couldn't untie was their lifeline.
The leash that no one untied was their lifeline.

Two dogs, arriving at the solidly frozen Styx
tear at the leash...

with frozen mouths unable even to bark

sever... the leash.

Moaning and crying,

making the icicles filling their mouths

a knife.

An eye-opener

The dead cat lay half buried.
Someone, unable to just pass by,
must have hastily half covered it.

That person must have known
that someone else, also unable to just pass by,
would cover the other half of the grave.

I have no idea who the person was
who first felt moved to make this grave.
Like indifferent grave diggers we both dug up soil
with sticks,
  collected it in the palm of our hands, scattered it.

Azaleas swaying in the mountain wind

briefly seemed to be offering condolences.

It was early spring, but it was cold, so I gathered reeds to cover it,

finally laid a flat stone without an inscription on it.

Just as rituals always come at unexpected moments,

we also make graves for unknown strangers

then leave without sorrowing.

They say that in the desert, a camel's carcass served as a signpost.

Only death showed the way.

What sign will this small-boned creature become?

No tears, wailing, or mourners, but although

in its lifetime we never met, it awakens these eyes.

Good times

A magpie and a crow often ate a late breakfast
as they rummaged through a dung heap together.
White and black things, vari-colored things
with different voices, eating and playing together,
they didn't fight, so they were unlike other species.

I was lazy
but as I picked up unsightly garbage in the forest
and became the master of the forest,
I used to enjoy the evenings when I came home
after hugging pine trees and throwing acorns
into the deeper forest.

I came to recognize the sound of trees crying.
The forest was tossed and turned all night long by

typhoons.

House prices are rising day by day
and in a house built with diagonal lines
I became lonely and crooked
like a broken oak tree)

There was nowhere a Paradise
like an untraded birds' nest
I was shaken by the world,
the tree was shaken by the wind,
but neither of us was uprooted.

Autumn came and the forest moved a little farther
away
like people who were once close leaving without a

word.

 The trees moved further apart
 and emitted a sound of red-eyed crying
 with the sound of grasshoppers.

 Things close by that had been far away,
 Things far away that had been close,

 When I left the forest one snowy day
 I thought I knew
 how big and green
 hornbeam leaves were,
 how big and pathetic the cicadas were,
 pulling their earlobes and crying in crowds.

What a huge tree you were,

what a pathetic wind swept to and fro, shook and
ceased,

why I flung down beautiful days.

I conceal

Faces

People

Love

Emotions

Food

Light

Heart

Kindness

Religion

Politics

Poetry

Song.

I conceal

with bias and

prejudice

with a discretion

that simply cannot be proved.

After concealing

concealing,

barely

I gain

Friends

Intuitions

one vague line of writing,

a messed-up

map

POET'S ESSAY

Finding my own ability

When moving bones

It was probably when I was about eighteen. I walked with Father, sweating profusely, along a mountain path that would normally take an hour even at a brisk pace. Since it was a season when people rarely used it, the mountain path was tangled with lush grass and vines. Loaded on the A-frame were two shovels, a sickle, a cloth and a plank. First, the grass on the grave mound, which had begun to grow thick, was cut with the sickle, and then the grave was dug up, like a scene from a horror movie. I probably did most of the shoveling. After digging for a while, two coffins were exposed. One belonged to my grandfather, whom I had never seen, and the other belonged to my grandmother, who died when I was six and I only vaguely remembered her face. Although they were a couple, the difference between their birth and death dates was close to 50 years. The bones were quickly recognizable as whose they were. We collected together the bones of different colors as reverently and neatly as possible. We removed the soil or foreign substances from between the bones with our bare hands, placed them on the pinewood board, and tied them with the cotton cloth. I did as Father told me. My grandmother's shroud had not fully rotted, and threads like fine fishing lines were wrapped around all her bones. I tried to remove them one by one, but the countless threads stuck in the gaps of the joints, would not come out easily, and could not be completely removed. Perhaps because of poverty, they must have been deceived and chosen a cheap one, a fake shroud made of nylon. As I go on living today, I often find those tough threads on my mind. We carried the remains of our ancestors to the main road on the A-frame. Father was unwell, so he gasped continuously, and he helped mainly with his mouth. I heard a pheasant crow on the mountain ahead. It was one day in early June that remains in my memory. Memories are things that are sometimes stored as sounds, temperatures, smells, or images. I did the job as if I was accustomed to it, but it wasn't something I was used to at all. Handling the tools was not difficult, but for the first time in my life, I was dealing with the body of a dead person, and I dug with fear and trembling, thinking that I was also dealing with souls. Perhaps at night, or alone, I wouldn't have been able to do it. I just have the normal courage allowing me to feel indifferent when I pass a house in mourning or a graveyard. It's not that I'm afraid of the living, but I used to feel fear of the dead and traditional tales. If those bones had not been blood relatives, if I had been hired to do that to earn money, I would not have been able to do it. Perhaps it was because I felt sure that they would not harm me with any spiritual or physical force. After a brief glimpse of the sun for the first time in decades, the bones were again buried in soft, sun-bathed soil. Moving those ancestors' bones seemed to lighten my mind about how lonely and dark it was in the shadowy mountains that could only be reached by walking over several hills. For the first time I saw and touched fleshless skulls and chill bones. Digging up, collecting, and moving those pitiful bones that were still in fetters may have matured me a little. Life is something we have to live by sensing and remembering certain lives and beings.

When moving rooms

My son, who is three years older than I was when

I went up to Seoul, wanted to live alone, so he moved out. Unexpectedly, what had been the room where my son lived became my room. Having moved to a room with an eastward-facing window, I could no longer hear the grotesque music rising until dawn from the floor below. Outside the window, instead of a uniform apartment wall, high and low houses lay spread out like a book. Perhaps given as an extra gift, a number of graceful mountain peaks could be seen to the east. On the day I helped him move to a rented room across the river, with his small amount of luggage packed in, I looked in the rear-view mirror and saw following us his childhood face, his cute tricks, his innocent tone, and the passing of time. The child who had felt so light when I gave him a ride on my shoulders was running behind the wheels. Tears came to my eyes because this too was a kind of parting. I reflected fleetingly that most roads follow waterways and the flowing water and the person who went flowing away will come back one day. I wondered whether to throw away or tie in bundles the worn-out comic books and children's books that my child had enjoyed as a child, but finally I put them on the bookshelf as memories. One wall was black where his back and head had rested on the wall, showing how dependent on the wall the child was, or how much fun he had. This mark was like the trace of time, of a family, that should not be erased but should rather be protected. It seems that there is not a single minute when human beings live without thinking, except when sleeping. And I always see people in my dreams while sleeping. There was never a time, whether I was lying down or standing up, when no face or memory was floating around. Rather than thinking about work or what to write, the faces of countless people come to mind more often. The chronic disease of having a good memory is both tiring and fortunate. Because of that chronic disease, nothing ever stays permanently or leaves completely.

However, perhaps because shifting my things to my son's room was also a kind of moving, I was feeling tired. I opened the window and gently closed my eyes, intending to listen to music, and let the fatigue go away... It was a gentle smile. It must have been the joy of owning that I was finally freed from a shared space and had my own room. It seemed to work well when I opened the window wide, turned on music, read a book, and wrote this and that. I gave my son independence reluctantly, and my son showed filial piety unintentionally. I don't think I've ever tried to get the good things in life first. It seems that I have been living convinced that it was cowardly to order other people to do things I didn't want to do. When I'm sending a manuscript I write a biography, but there is not much to write. I try to extend it a bit, but then an awkward feeling comes and I shorten it again. When I saw people writing lengthy biographies, I was both envious and puzzled about their pride. Poetry is the beauty of compression, but I wondered if a biography should be longer than one poem. To me, the past is like a manuscript with a lot of typos and grammatical errors that needs to be proofread. This is probably because errors and mistakes, inertia and boredom, are intertwined with time. It's not all, but the more I read what I have written, the more it wearies me. These days, I am trying to live in a state where there is no gravity, no sense of restraint or duty. I didn't realize that I was so good at quitting what I was doing. I'm starting to lose my conviction that going straight, challenging, or maintaining a situation is what protects my identity. Knowing how to be resigned or be skeptical is also part of courage, of self-defense. I feel dissatisfied with my poems, which are not so very short. There is a myth that if there is strength, the breath of a poem grows longer, but it seems that my energy decreases every year, and if the poems are too short, there is a feeling that the price of the book is excessive.

Finding the strength

After publishing a book of poetry, the way ahead unfolding before your eyes becomes a labyrinth or a blank page. If sorrow is what makes poetry poetry, sad things cannot be made to order, and if poetry comes only when you are hungry, you cannot enjoy the kind of life that you have worked so hard for. Dramatic events don't burst out or come running. Although it is an intuition based on experience, poverty is not high, and those who do not want to lose human dignity and shame under any conditions are high. I have seen a lot of shabbiness in poverty and it seems that I have experienced a lot of discord. There are few people without any kind of desire, and while acknowledging that we are worldly, flawed and greedy beings, we strive to live in a slightly different way, and I think that those who have a will for symbiosis and cooperation are relatively high beings. Those who have tried to understand far and deep without making hasty decisions seemed to be intellectually high. People who looked at identity first rather than heterogeneity were gentle and easy to approach. Wasn't poetry, after all, a process and a result of discernment? Just as it is not easy to distinguish a person from a situation, choosing what is poetic is not always difficult or simple. It is accompanied by misunderstandings and errors.

The poems did not come by themselves, just as the sun naturally rises in the east, so I had no choice but to become a magnet. I tried to find objects or narratives to stick to, but the scope of the work was not wide. I didn't have the energy or the heart to travel far. Those bits of scrap iron were not in the air. But this is only half true. Poetry was something that had to be able to attract things like air, wind, breath, ideas, and non-ferrous metals. It was obliged to transfer magnetism to beings without magnetism, making them stick to each other. Sometimes you have to push it out and finally let it live on its own. The things that stuck to me were on the ground, by the water, in the grass, on peoples' forehead, hearts. There were even many on tombs. There were dogs and grasshoppers, and there were rice fields and soybean fields that were more beautiful than flowerbeds. It's not that I didn't suffer from the things I lived for, but I wouldn't say that I suffered more than others. Because they were common and lacked inspiration, such daily routines did not appear on their own. Labor lasting for more than 30 years kept us alive, but it was also boring and did not seem to contain any distinctive material. Nevertheless, I am in favor of poets who sweat outside of writing. That ordinary living environment may be the mother of an imagination that is not lonely and empty. Even if it cannot be a direct poem right now, it may be the central axis supporting their efforts. And poetic things may be getting in the way, in the midst of the unfaithfulness of living slowly and wastefully, outside the non-standard tracks, in the roaming blanks.

Lying flat on the floor

Whether it's strange or fortunate, the days when writing was being done were not days of deep hardship or pain, but days of being generous and calm. Like the light that likes to appear when there are no clouds. When something is cleared up, the desire to write arises. Therefore, long quarrels with the beings with whom I had to live were the enemies of writing. I had to become a human being who even pretended to be a peace-oriented person by controlling myself. Among the things attached to the magnetic force of me, there are no shiny metal pieces. Faces like black iron powder or faces that have disappeared, passions and emotions from microhistory. They had to be made into sentences that somehow connected the earth, water, wood, oxidized bones, lost time and weight. What do you gain from writing poetry? Some might say freedom, but I felt like I was gaining in loss of freedom. It could not be said that there was no joy in the work, but in life and fate, it seemed that I gained incompetence. As I write, I will find a handful of honor that I never know when it will be destroyed, and that vain name will harass me and torment me. Nevertheless, as if I was lucky enough to get a room this size, I regard the path I have taken while living like this as luck or bliss. As writing continues, the eastern sky darkens first at sunset. Being ahead or being late is just an optical illusion. The time given to us, the total amount of joy and sorrow may be fair. In that sense, I like flat things, generous and optimistic hearts, and slow flowing water. Whether it is a person, an animal, or an object, I want to believe that they are beings who have good intentions and a hope of coexistence. It's impossible, but ultimately, I want to live in a place where there are no low-level fights. I will not forget to keep an eye on the bad guys. I always corrected poems facing west, but this time I write with a calm mind, lying on a bench, looking at the darkening eastern sky. Errors will surely come in future. A blank sheet to be faced with embarrassment.

The toil or joy
of continuing life and poetry

Kim Su-yee (Literary Critic)

Moon Dong-man is right. Poetry is a product
of desire, a maze of discernment. No matter how
much is emptied out and removed, if there was
no desire, not a single word or sentence would
have been written in the first place. The maze of
discernment is dizzying in the land of poetry, where
all kinds of desires churning and bloom—novelty,
aesthetics, emotion, ethics, originality, literary
value, recognition of others, fame, etc. The various
and different names for 'desire' and 'discernment'
also boast of literary sophistication. Even the
'indifference' without desire and the 'indifference',
which have been praised by many poets since the

birth of literature, are no exception to this list. For a person who is without desire and indifferent will not seek language, nor will they feel the need to express themselves in language. It is the same as saying that although there are words that refer to freedom from desire and indifference, there are no words that are freedom from desire and indifference in themselves. Even including the words 'freedom from desire' and 'indifference'.

To Moon Dong-man, continuing poetry is the same as continuing life. Unless liberated, a person cannot completely abandon desires and live. The same goes for writing poetry. Desire, which is human nature, is the energy that makes life and poetry spring up and grow. Desire in itself is neither good nor bad. Therefore, the problem is not desire itself, but the attitude, object, method, and use of desire. The key to the life and poetry of a human-poet lies in how to control one's own desires, and what to create and achieve through those desire and share that with others. Thus, what unfolds in the poetry is the world of 'discernment' that rises toward a higher and more beautiful dimension, full of the energy, vigor, and joy of living beings.

In this collection of poems, Moon Dong-man gives insight into the 'time of connection', a common attribute of life and poetry, through the lens of 'desire'. He outlines a narrative of life from his grandparents to his own children in this one volume of poetry. The fifties, which are the age the poet is now passing through, offer an opportunity for such insight. The fifties is generally the age at which a person is closer to their death than to their birth. They are an age at which they have experienced and learned many times that the desires of life, in a word, cannot overcome time and collapse in the face of death. At the same time, Moon Dong-man also talks about the opposite fact or truth, that life will continue past the death of 'me', and that poetry too will continue past the death of 'me'. Life unfolds on its own in many moments, regardless of human will, and poetry, too, in many cases goes its own way regardless of the poet's intentions. Perhaps the initiative in life and poetry lies not in 'I' but in life and poetry. That is because life is both an unknown impossibility and an open possibility that I cannot fully control or predict.

"Thanks to the people going to prepare rice, we just about managed to stay alive," ("Cooking Rice"). According to Moon Dong-man, the reason humans can continue their lives is thanks to "people going to prepare rice." In this simple and sharp insight, the key lies not in the 'rice', but in the 'people' who prepare the meal. Those who prepare the meals are those who feed themselves and feed others. According to Moon Dong-man's childhood memories, traditional Korean society has been passed down by those who cook rice from above, along with those who owe them rice (life). A grandfather whose face he never saw, a grandmother who took care of her baby when her daughter-in-law gave birth, a father who dug up his parents' graves with his 18-year-old son and moved them to another spot, a mother who cultivated a vegetable garden until she died to feed her children, poor people who devoted their lives to cultivating a few small fields, people who were unjustly victims of the violence of tragic history, and so on.

Moon Dong-man describes the history of the people who prepared the rice, the people who depended on them, and the life they achieved together. "Things that keep going, things that make you want to sit together while peeping around, things that keep you from leaving." Life is what connects people who are connected to each other.

Even after the world changes and the relationship ends, people's connections and the connections of life continue in another form. This is because the heart that someone possesses, wanting to be with them, and can't leave, passes lightly beyond physical limits. Moon Dong-man brings those days and people into the present through his memories and love. Memory and love are powerful forces that connect distant beings over time and place. Moon Dong-man summons the ways of 'living linked together' and 'living together' from the traditional Korean society of the past, and transforms that into the current ethics that we must live in a hellish reality. "If there is someone who prays for me one day when I am at a crossroads barefoot and trembling in fear... I will pray for you even if I go to hell. How could there be no crack in hell?"

A prayer for someone unknown in a crack of hell! It would not be wrong to say that that is a metaphorical explanation of how Moon Dong-man's poetry is born. In the gaps of the hell called reality, Mun Dongman feels the warmth of people as he sees scenes from a world that has passed but will never disappear completely. As someone who continues life together as an individual, and as a poet who continues to write poetry together as an individual, Moon Dong-man summarizes his tasks as follows: "(It) is not a question of what might be passed on, not a question of how to make a leap forward while living and writing, but rather a matter of going on writing without collapsing." (Continuing Days). That is the core of life and poetry.

K-POET
Thinking Less about Sad Things

Written by Moon Dong-man
Translated by Brother Anthony of Taizé
Published by ASIA Publishers
Address 445, Hoedong-gil, Paju-si, Gyeonggi-do, Korea
Tel (8231).955.7958
Fax (8231).955.7956
Email bookasia@hanmail.net
Homepage Address www.bookasia.org

ISBN 979-11-5662-317-5 (set) | 979-11-5662-593-3 (04810)
First published in Korea by ASIA Publishers 2022

This book is published with the support of the Literature Translation Institute of Korea
(LTI Korea).